American Sign Language

A B C D E F G H I J K L M

"You can discover more about a person in an hour of play than in a year of conversation."

-Plato

N O P Q R S T U V W X Y Z

A CLUE FOR YOU:

TAIL IN THE TEAPOT

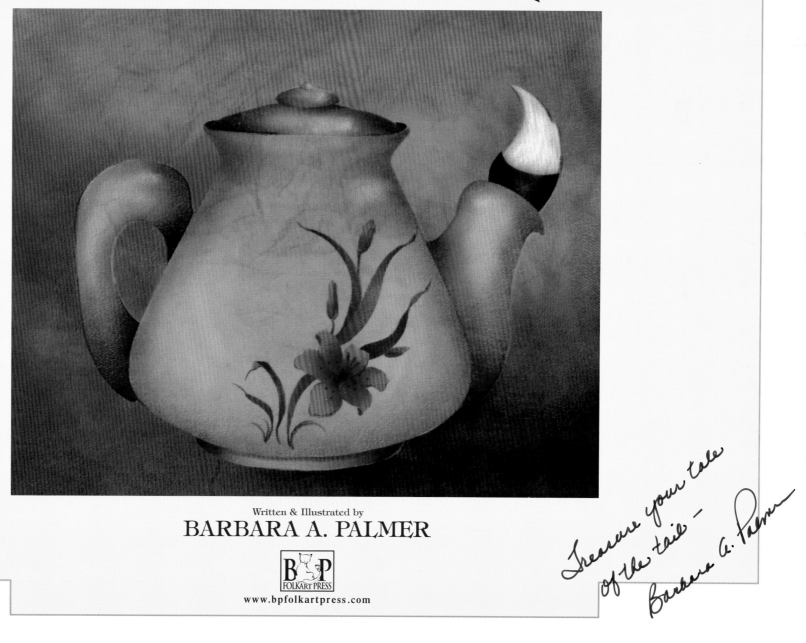

Written & Illustrated by
BARBARA A. PALMER

BP
FOLKART PRESS

www.bpfolkartpress.com

Treasure your tale
of the tail —
Barbara A. Palmer

Contents of this book also include:
American Sign Language and Alphabet and
Children's Activities

Art: Theorem paintings by Barbara A. Palmer
For more information on theorem painting go to

www.bpfolkartpress.com

Font: Display type set in Mambo, text type in Timbrel and sign language in Gallaudet

Photography: Neil Montanus
Graphic design: Barbara A. Palmer and David Beadling
Editing: Jetze Beers
Copyright: 2007
Published: 2007 China
First Edition

ISBN 978-0-9728228-2-4
Library of Congress Control Number: 2007900905
1. American Sign Language - Juvenile Fiction
2. Animals - Juvenile Fiction
3. Flowers- Juvenile Fiction
4. Friendship - Juvenile Fiction
5. Game - Juvenile Fiction
6. Rhymed Text - Juvenile Fiction
7. Sleuth Story - Juvenile Fiction

Summary: Rhymed text. A floral themed sleuth story with finger-spelled clues in
American Sign Language. A rescue. A friendship.

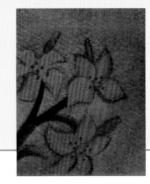

Paintings are flowers I grow to share with others.

In memory of my friend Lonna DeRoo

Other books created by Barbara A. Palmer:

The Journey of Cattail

ISBN 0972822801
9780972822800

Finding Fido the Feline

Flip Book with American Sign Language

ISBN 097282281X
9780972822817

A portion of the proceeds from the sale of this book will be donated to The Humane Society.

1

**A** game began one golden summery morning at Fanny Flowerbed's Farm.

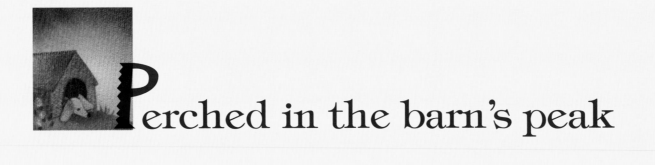

Perched in the barn's peak

was F i d o the Feline.

His long tail flicked to and fro,

while his playmate, W i l l i a m

the Watchdog, napped below.

Suddenly...

4

Fido, feeling like fun, scampered out of the barn and flew by the startled William. "Hide and seek! You're it!" squealed the fleeing feline.

A long, black tail with a white tip was all William saw as Fido passed under a flapping quilt. William pranced in pursuit.

6

"Where is Fido? Where is my friend Fido?" woofed the wondering watchdog.

"Three clues for you, only one is true," Geranium Goose giddily replied.

Tail in the teapot,
Tail in the trumpet vine,
Tail in the tablecloth.

(William failed to see Fido, do you?

These fingers spell your clue: 👊✊☝️👌✊)

"Oh where…" William whined,
still treading Fido's trail.

"Three clues for you, only one is true,"
thumped Bluebell Bunny.

Tail in the touch-me-nots,
Tail in the tiger lily,
Tail in the tomatoes.

(William failed to see Fido, do you?
Clue: 👊👊✋👊✋👊✋)

"**L**isten to me," laughed Laurel Lamb,
"Three clues for you, only one is true."

Tail in the treetop,
Tail in the tiny toolshed,
Tail in the turnips.

(William failed to see Fido, do you?
Clue: 🤟🤚✊☝️👉✋)

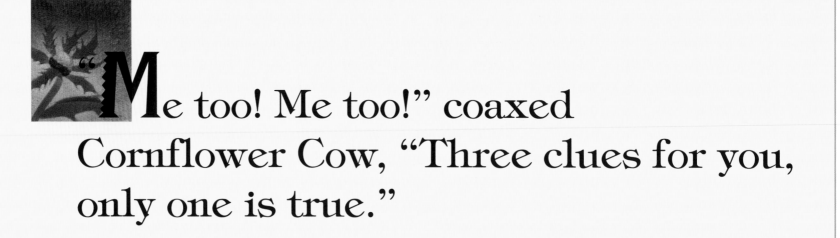

"Me too! Me too!" coaxed
Cornflower Cow, "Three clues for you,
only one is true."

Tail in the thistles,
Tail in the timothy,
Tail on Turkey Foot Trail.

(William failed to see Fido, do you?
Clue:)

"My turn! My turn!" squeaked Fern the Field Mouse, "Three clues for you, only one is true."

Tail in the trillium,
Tail in the toadstools,
Tail in the thimbleberries.

(William failed to see Fido, do you?
Clue: )

"I'm next! I'm next!" beckoned
Buttercup the Butterfly,
"Three clues for you, only one is true."

Tail in the tansies,
Tail in the timber,
Tail in the tulip tree.

(William failed to see Fido, do you?
Clue: )

"Olly Molly Oxen Free, tapioca just for me!" nickered Molly Morgan Horse, "I like tapioca, I do. Three clues for you, only one is true."

Tail in the tea rose,
Tail in the thorn apple,
Tail in the tasty tapioca.

(William failed to see Fido, do you?
Clue: )

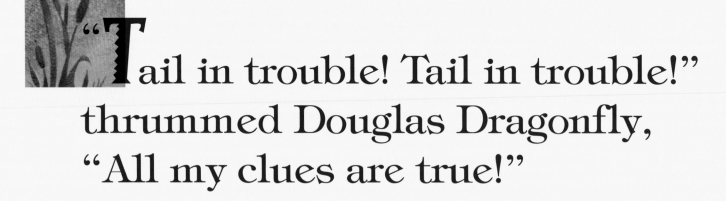

"Tail in trouble! Tail in trouble!"
thrummed Douglas Dragonfly,
"All my clues are true!"

Fido's fallen near the turtle,
near the tadpoles,
in the nearby trout pond!

(William sees Fido, do you?
Clue: 🤟👊👊👊✌️👆👊)

21

"In a flash, William dashed and splashed, to pluck his playmate to safety.

"Fun loving felines are not freshwater fish!" woofed the watchdog.

Fido purred a playful reply:
Twilight has come,
our clue game is done.
Did you have fun?

(William's tail waggled a sign for: 🤙✊✊)

That night, William's lantern eyes watched Fido's tail dance with fireflies, under the moonlit sky.

Friends forever.

CHILDREN'S ACTIVITIES

Description of plants and flowers found in this book.
Some are used as first names for characters in the story.

   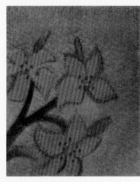

Bluebell:
A blue, bell-shaped woodland flower with strap like leaves.

Cattail:
Found in swamps and ponds. Grows very tall with a long, brown, furry spike.

Fern:
A shade plant that has slender lace like fronds.

Tiger Lily:
Large trumpet shaped flower, orange-red with black dots.